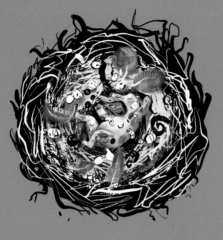

BIRD BOY

A GRIMM AND GROSS RETELLING

BY BENJAMIN HARPER

ILLUSTRATED BY TIMOTHY BANKS

raintree

a Capstone company — pu

D1347793

CONTENTS

WARNING!

This retelling of "The Foundling-Bird" gets a bit grim and gross at times. Keep an eye (and nose) out for the disgusting lunches at the park ranger station, but try not to lose your own lunch. Once you're feeling better, read on. You'll find out that even if you have special powers, magic is not always pretty! Yuck!

 = # GRIM

The Grimm brothers were known for writing some *GRIM* tales. Look for the thumbs-down and you'll know the story is about to get grim.

 = # GROSS

Luckily there's also a lot of *GROSS* stuff in this story. Look for the thumbs-up to see when it's about to get gross.

---

 1. These are footnotes. Get it? Dr Grossius Grimbus, researcher of all things grim and gross, shares his highly scientific observations.

CHAPTER ONE
BABY ON A BRANCH!

Once upon a time, there was a kindly
forest ranger called Dan. One morning, he
walked into the dining area at the ranger
station where he worked. He almost passed
out from the smell.

Rotting cabbage, sweaty feet, dirty nappies
and fish. All these odours were wrapped up
into one big, nasty smell. It had taken over
the entire building. He was used to the cook's
awful meals. But today's odour was one of the
worst ever.

FLUMPF!

Sanna the cook dumped a glob of bubbling green goo onto his plate. The goo was filled with pink chunks.

GURGLE! GURGLE!

A string of bubbly slime trailed behind as the cook lifted her spoon off his plate.

Sanna was a terrible cook. Sometimes the rangers thought they might be eating vomit. But she had been working there for so long. No one had the heart to sack her.

Besides, the rangers worked hard all day out in the forest. They were always hungry. Plates of stinky slime were better than nothing.

"Thank you," Ranger Dan said. He eyed the jiggling goo. He didn't want to hurt her feelings. "This just looks delicious!"

Ranger Dan lived at the remote Dark Woods Station with his baby daughter, Cassie. The other forest rangers and their families lived there too.

When Dan had finished eating, he went out to check on some saplings. It was part of his job to grow baby trees. The rangers had to replant a big area of forest that had been lost to a fire. Dan loved his job very much.

As he was hiking, Dan heard the strangest sound. It was coming from way up in the top of a tree! At first it sounded like someone passing really loud gas. But when Dan got closer, he stopped in his tracks. It sounded like a baby! A *human* baby!

Ranger Dan took a pair of binoculars out of his pack and looked up. High in the tree was a gigantic bird's nest. The sound kept coming. He had to climb up and be sure!

Up and up he climbed until he reached the top of the tree.

"What on earth?!"

In the centre of the gigantic nest lay a little baby. The baby was covered in feathers, dried worm guts and poo. He rocked back and forth and screamed. This was the weirdest baby Dan had ever seen. Instead of a nose, he had a little yellow beak! "You poor little guy. How'd you get up here?" Dan asked.

Dan knew he had to take that baby home. If he didn't, the baby might end up as food for some giant bird. He carefully put the child in his backpack. Then he shimmied down the tree.

When he got back to the station, Ranger Dan called the police to report the found baby.

Many weeks passed. But no parents came forward to claim the child. Dan decided to adopt the baby, who was about the same age as Cassie.

Dan looked lovingly at the baby with the beak for a nose. "I'll call you Birdy!" he exclaimed.

CHAPTER TWO
BUBBLING IN THE POT

Birdy had refused to eat Sanna's food as a toddler. Ranger Dan agreed that the food was gross. But the boy had to eat something! He let Cassie and Birdy find food for Birdy each day in the forest. They gathered apples and bird's eggs and wild blueberries. And once in a while they'd find a fat, juicy worm.

As Birdy grew older, he learned to eat Sanna's cooking along with everyone else.

Birdy also realized he had a special talent. One day when he and Cassie were playing in the woods, he accidentally turned a mushroom into a toad. He could do magic! Over the years the children would laugh and laugh as he transformed pine cones and rocks into all kinds of creatures.

But Birdy's magic would soon cause him problems. One morning when the children were a bit older, they were playing outside the kitchen. Birdy turned a turnip into a monkey. He and Cassie laughed and played with the magical creature. When they looked up, they saw Sanna gazing at them through the kitchen window. She gave them an evil smile before going back to her cooking.

From then on, they were both terrified of Sanna. They did everything to avoid her. After all, she served them awful food. Even worse, she looked like a witch!

Birdy was especially wary of her. He often caught Sanna glaring at him. Sometimes she would scribble in an old book that had SPELLS written across the cover.

Birdy was convinced the cook was planning something horrible for him. When he told his dad, the ranger had just laughed. "She is harmless. I promise!"

"Here you go, dears," Sanna said on Birdy's eleventh birthday.[1] She ladled out heaped helpings of green foam. It smelled like a sewer. "I made this just for you. It's liver, spinach and tripe casserole! Happy birthday!"

The cook dumped the horrible, awful-smelling glop onto Birdy's plate.

Birdy and Cassie sat down at a table. They pushed the food around their plates.

1. They had no real way of knowing Birdy's birthday, since he had been found in a tree, so they just celebrated each year on the date he was found.

"This dish tastes like a compost heap," Birdy said. He plugged his nose at the green goop on his plate. "And this salad tastes like dirty socks and rotten eggs." He swatted flies away with his fork.

Birdy felt Sanna staring at him from across the room. He looked up and saw her cold, heartless gaze. "She's a witch. I just know it," Birdy told Cassie. "I won't eat another bite she cooks. I bet it's poisoned, or has a spell on it, or worse!"

One night Cassie couldn't sleep and needed a drink of water. She sneaked very quietly into the kitchen. As she filled her glass, she noticed a glow coming from behind the cracked door to the storage room. She tiptoed over and peeked inside.

Cassie saw a room full of candles, a giant cauldron and loads of old books. The shelves were full of powders and herbs. There were racks of what looked like dried guts.

Sanna stood over the giant cauldron stirring a disgusting blend.

I hope that isn't breakfast, thought Cassie.

Sanna looked very excited. She spoke to her two assistants, Gristle and Toby, and dumped some black powder into the mix. "Now that

he is eleven, I can finally make my magic potion!" Sanna cackled.

 This is where things get pretty GROSS. . . .

Sanna threw a handful of mould into the pot. Then she tossed in twenty-five rotten eggs, a few tins of black tar and 16 cups of dead flies. To top it off, Sanna sifted in dried things that Cassie thought looked like scabs. The mess in that cauldron smelled horrific. Cassie pinched her nostrils to keep from vomiting.

And here's where things begin to get fairly **GRIM**. . . .

"That nasty little Birdy is the final ingredient," Sanna hissed. She read from the yellowed pages of an old, leather-bound recipe book. "'Bones of a magical boy, aged eleven, born with the beak of a bird, who was found in a tree.' I never thought I would come across such a rare ingredient. Yet here he is! I'm going to boil him in this pot. I'll bleach his bones in the sun and grind them up into powder. Then I can make the ultimate Fluffy Seven-Layer Beaky Bird Boy Meringue Cake for Ranger Dan's birthday. And he'll never know what he's eating!"

Cassie gasped. What else had they been eating all these years?

"In order for the spell to work, it must be eaten. Every last crumb! Then the spell will give me ultimate power over whatever I desire! I will be queen of the forest. I will rule it as I see fit! All who enter it will bow to me!" She cackled, raising her hands over the bubbling cauldron. "Make sure you save the leftover ingredients," she said to her assistants. "Who knows when skin, teeth or hair could come in handy?"

"Is that potion really going to work?" Toby asked.

"You dare to question me?" Sanna roared. She dipped her spoon into the muck. Then she splashed some of the mixture onto the ground. It sparked and exploded like a firecracker. Orange smoke billowed into the air.

"Yes, I'd say that works," Gristle murmured.

Sanna pointed a bony, wart-covered finger at her minions. "Tomorrow morning, climb up to the boy's nest as soon as Ranger Dan leaves for work. Snatch him up. Then bring him here as quietly as you can. We'll throw him in the pot and boil him down to jelly!"

Her assistants chuckled. Cassie quivered behind the door. Then she tiptoed away as quickly as she could.

CHAPTER THREE
INTO THE FOREST!

Cassie got no sleep that night. She tossed and turned. Sanna planned to boil her brother in order to take control of the forest. She couldn't let it happen. Before dawn Cassie jumped out of bed and got dressed.

She climbed up the ladder to the roof where Birdy had his special bed. Ranger Dan had made it out of tree branches, roots and the stuffing from old pillows. Birdy always said that he couldn't sleep unless he was up high.

"Get up!" she said, shaking Birdy awake. "We are in big trouble! Remember how you said Sanna was planning something? It's worse than you thought! Get dressed quickly!"

Birdy stared at her, not knowing what to do.

"MOVE IT!" Cassie shouted. "Sanna is a witch! She's got a crazy scheme to become queen of the forest. One of the main ingredients in her spell is, well, YOU!"

Birdy couldn't believe it. He thought Cassie was joking. "Come on, that's just silly," he said. He was about to turn over, pull the feather blanket back up and go back to sleep.

But then Cassie started to cry. And that's when Birdy knew she was telling the truth.

"You're not joking, are you? I'm sorry," he said to his sister. "Let's get out of here!" Birdy jumped out of bed and got dressed faster than he ever had before.

"Bone bleaching does not sound fun at all!" He threw on his shoes. "And I don't even like meringue. I certainly don't want to BE one!" They climbed down the ladder and began to sneak through the grounds of the ranger station.

Suddenly Ranger Dan appeared from behind a shed. He'd been gathering some tools to take with him into the forest.

"You kids OK?" he asked. He was surprised to see them up and about so early.

"Yes, Dad," Cassie replied as her father headed towards the station, probably for his breakfast. "We're hoping to see some baby raccoons before they go to sleep for the day."

Birdy was about to say something about Sanna's plan when Cassie stomped on his foot. "Ouch!" he said, jumping up and down. "Why'd you do that?"

"Sanna's a witch! Who knows what she'll do if we tell on her? We've got to get out of here. Then we can come up with a plan!"

Birdy and Cassie sneaked into the woods. When they looked back, they saw Sanna opening the door to her back room. She grabbed a basket full of bright yellow toadstools. Behind her, the giant black cauldron bubbled more furiously than it had the night before! Green foam formed peaks above a boiling hot mixture.

"She wants to put me in THAT?" Birdy whispered. He looked terrified.

"Just remember, never leave me and I'll never leave you," Cassie said.

"Yes!" Birdy said. "We will stick together!"

And with that they headed into the dark and mysterious forest.

CHAPTER FOUR
MAGIC MOMENTS

"Oh, my pot is boiling.

And into it I'll throw

some lipids, tendons, skin and teeth,

a finger, ear and toe!"

Sanna sang her happy song as she stirred her disgusting mixture.

SPLOSH!

It was almost the right consistency.[2] She sprinkled some dried slug mucus over it as a final touch. "There! All ready for that little brat's bones!" She clapped her hands,

---

2. It looked like a lanced boil. Or maybe maggots.

summoning her assistants. "You know what to do," she said calmly. "Bring that child here and dump him in the pot. Once I have power, you, too, shall reap a great reward!"

Gristle and Toby scampered away to do her bidding.

As she sat there reviewing the spell, they burst back into the room.

"Birdy is gone!" Toby shouted, out of breath. "And the girl is gone as well!"

Sanna panicked. What if the two little monsters had found out about her plan? They would tell Ranger Dan. She could go to prison! She would never rule the forest!

"Run after them! If I know those little brats, I bet they went into the forest!

Search everywhere and bring those children back to me!"

Luckily Birdy and Cassie's father had taught them all sorts of survival tricks. They knew how to build shelters, make fires and purify water. They could even forage for food. They could survive for days if they had to.

Cassie knew they should hike alongside the stream. That way they'd always have fresh water nearby. Birdy picked any edible berries and nuts he saw along their route. They had been walking quickly for quite a while when they decided it was safe to take a little rest.

"I'm so tired," Cassie breathed. They sat down on the forest floor.

"What are we going to do?" Birdy said. "We can't just run forever."

Just then they heard footsteps.

"Those little creeps can't have got too far," they heard someone say.

Birdy and Cassie jumped up. They looked around for a place to hide. The men were getting closer.

"There! I see them!" Toby pointed. "I see the top of Birdy's head behind that stump!"

"Quick, stand next to me!" Birdy said to Cassie. "I haven't tried my magic on people yet, but it's our only hope!"

Cassie's eyes opened wide.

"Don't worry. Just trust me!" Birdy said. "I'll turn into a rosebush and turn you into a rose. They won't be able to do anything to us then!"

"You'll turn me into what?!" Cassie replied.

Quickly, Birdy clapped his hands. A puff of smoke surrounded the two children. When it cleared there was . . .

A pig snorting in a mud puddle.

"Huh?" Gristle said. "Where'd they go?"

"They were here, all right," Toby said. He pointed to a pile of food Birdy had gathered.

The pig looked at them.

"Hey, wait a minute. That pig knows something!" Gristle said.

"What are you, crazy? It's a pig! And what's a pig doing in the middle of the woods?"

Gristle shrugged. The two stormed back towards the station to report their findings.

Once they were gone, the pig snorted. *SNOOORT!*

And a moment later, there were Birdy and Cassie, covered in mud.

"You call that a rosebush?" Cassie yelled. "I'm all dirty!"

"I don't get to practise very often," Birdy replied. "Anyway, we're safe, aren't we?"

The two cleaned themselves off in the stream. Then they hiked further into the forest. They knew that Sanna would send her assistants back. And when she did, they needed to be far away from where the magic mud puddle had been!

When Toby and Gristle told her what they had seen, Sanna was not pleased. "You idiots! Have you ever seen a pig and a mud puddle in the middle of the forest? That boy is magic! Why do you think I want him for my recipe? Go back there and get that pig!"

So her assistants hiked back into the woods. When they came to where the mud puddle had been, they saw that it was gone. And so was the pig!

"Let's follow the stream," Toby said. "That's what any good camper would do. We'll catch up to those children. We're much faster than they are!"

Sure enough, as they climbed over a hill in the forest, the men saw Birdy and Cassie in the distance.

"Get them!" Gristle shouted. They rushed towards the two children.

Birdy and Cassie heard the men coming from far away.

"Here we go again," Cassie said. "What are you going to turn me into this time – a rubbish bin?"

"I'll turn into a cabin. I'll turn you into a chandelier hanging in the middle of the room."

"Weird, but OK! I'm ready!" Cassie said.

POOF!

There on the tree was a tiny little bird's nest, and inside it was a red robin.

CHIRP! CHIRP! Birdy couldn't help himself. He sang a sweet song. He watched as the men approached.

"They were right here!" Gristle said, picking his ear.

"I saw them too," Toby wheezed. He was out of breath from having to lug himself up the hill.

"Well there's nothing here now. Except for this stupid bird singing its annoying song," Gristle sputtered.

"Sanna won't be pleased if we tell her we lost them again," Toby hissed. "She might get angry and throw *us* into that nasty pot of hers!"

They thought about that. Over the years there *had* been people from the station who had just sort of disappeared. They both swallowed hard.

"Well, there's no use putting it off," said Gristle.

The men trudged back towards the station, dragging their feet.

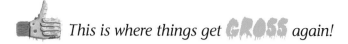 *This is where things get* **GROSS** *again!*

Cassie turned back into herself. "I'm covered in mites!" she exclaimed. "How did I go from being a chandelier to being a bird's nest? And look, I'm covered in poo! Couldn't you have waited?"

"Everyone knows birds can't control things like that!" Birdy said. His feelings were hurt.

"Obviously," Cassie said. "Come on! We don't have time to talk. Let's get going!"

* * *

"You fools!" Sanna screamed.

Toby and Gristle backed away from the witch.

Green slime bubbled up over the side of the cauldron and slid onto the floor.

Sanna stomped her foot. "Clearly I'm going to have to get this child myself!" She got her shawl and threw it over her shoulders. Then she turned to her assistants. "Now you two stay here. And keep stirring! If anything tries to crawl out, poke it down with that stick!"

Then she stormed out into the forest.

CHAPTER FIVE
BYE-BYE, WITCH!

"Those two dummies," Sanna seethed. She waddled into the woods. "I always end up having to do everything myself."

 Can you believe it gets **GRIMMER**?

The woods were dark. The trees twisted. Gnarled branches reached out. Even Sanna didn't like spending too much time there.

Luckily witches have a special ability.

They can sniff out children when they need them for recipes and such. Sanna used her nose to track Birdy and Cassie through the trees. She came upon the place where the mud had been. There she saw the children's muddy footprints leading off into the distance.

"I'll find you yet!" she screamed. "And when I do, you'll be thrown into the pot. And your little friend too! I am no longer Mrs Nice Witch!"

She kept going deeper and deeper into the forest. The trees grew thicker and thicker. Sunlight barely made it through. She crawled along with her nose close to the ground, picking up the children's scent. Even after she had accidentally sniffed a pile of deer droppings, she continued.

And then, she saw it – a clearing. The sun shone brightly down. There in the middle of the clearing were Birdy and Cassie.

"I have you now," she said. Just then, she stepped on a bundle of twigs.

CRUNCH!

She fell down.

"What was that?" Cassie cried. She looked towards the trees.

"Oh no. Look!" Birdy pointed. "It's Sanna!"

"I don't care what you turn me into this time. Just do it now!" Cassie said. She closed her eyes.

"OK, here goes!" Birdy concentrated. A gigantic cloud of smoke filled the clearing.

Sanna brushed twigs off herself as she stood up. She tried to see through the smoke. Leaves and sticks were stuck in her hair. A beetle had crawled up her nose. She pulled the bug out and shoved it into her pocket.

"I can use that later to spice up lunch," she said.

Then the smoke cleared.

"Aha," she said. "Trying to pull a fast one on me, are you?" Sanna walked out of the trees and came upon the shore of a small pond. She stroked her chin, thinking. "I know what you've done, Birdy. I'll build a fire and dry this pond out. You'll dry up till you're nothing but bones!"

She looked out over the water. "But wait. Where have you hidden your little friend?"

Sanna glanced around. She could find nothing out of the ordinary.

"Oh, well. I'll deal with her later!" Sanna cried. She pulled a wand out of her satchel. "Right now, it's your turn!"

But before she could wave her wand over the pond, the water started to stir.

She stared in awe. A plesiosaur in oddly familiar clothes lifted its head out of the water.

It swam over to the shore and bit down on Sanna's head. Then it dragged her into the murky depths of the pond.

CLAP!

A puff of smoke appeared. Then Birdy and Cassie were standing there all by themselves.

"But, where's Sanna?" Cassie squeezed water out of her shirt. She looked around where the pond had been. "What if she comes back?"

"She's down there," Birdy said. He pointed at the ground. "But we are safe for now. I put her in a cave. It will take her a while to dig herself out. We'll tell Dad what has been going on. And Sanna won't ever bother us again!"

Birdy and Cassie ran back to the ranger station. They were just in time to meet Ranger Dan coming home from work. When they told him what had happened, he radioed for the police. The police officers came and picked up Toby and Gristle.

They put an electrified fence around Dark Woods Station and hired a nice new cook. He cooked pancakes and sausage for breakfast and pizza for dinner.

And everyone lived happily ever after. . . . except for Sanna. She never got to make her evil potion. And, after digging herself out of the ground, she got lost in the forest forever.

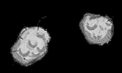

THE END

COMPARING THE TALES

The Brothers Grimms' story called "The Foundling-Bird" tells about a weird little boy found in a nest. He's not discovered by a park ranger, but instead he's found (which is why he is called a "foundling") by a man whose job is also connected with the forest – a woodcutter. Birdy is taken home with the woodcutter, grows up as a friend to the man's daughter and meets the disgusting Sanna – the witch-cook.

In the Grimms' version, we never really know why Sanna wants to cook poor Birdy's goose. Benjamin Harper's story gives an interesting explanation: Sanna needs the magical boy as a key ingredient for a potion that will make her ruler of the forest. That seems to be a pretty good reason. If you're a witch, that is.

About Birdy's magical transformations that disguise Cassie and him as they flee from Sanna – well, in the Grimms' story, the magic works perfectly. Ben's version, however, makes more sense. Birdy hasn't had a lot of practice casting spells, so naturally something will go wrong.

How about the part of Benjamin's story with his gross and revolting descriptions of Sanna's terrible cooking? His language is really vivid. Sanna "ladled out heaped helpings of green foam" that "smelled like a sewer". We hope you didn't read this story just after lunch. Sorry if so! But if you didn't, please warn the next person. And make sure your school isn't serving stewed tomatoes for lunch that day!

GLOSSARY

cauldron large kettle, often associated with witches' brews

chandelier light fixture that hangs from the ceiling and is usually lit by small lights

consistency how thick or thin something is

edible able to be eaten

forage search for food in the wild

plesiosaur large swimming reptile that lived during the time of the dinosaurs

purify remove any dirty or harmful substances

satchel bag sometimes carried over the shoulder

scampered ran lightly and quickly

shimmied moved or shook your body from side to side

sputtered made spitting noises

GROSSARY

BOIL painful, swollen spot on the body that is usually caused by an infection

COMPOST HEAP mixture of rotted leaves, vegetables, manure and other items that are added to soil to make it richer

DROPPINGS animal poo

MITE tiny creature with eight legs that is related to the spider

MUCUS sticky or slimy fluid that coats and protects the inside of the nose, throat, lungs and other parts of the body

ODOUR smell

ROTTING something that is decaying

SCAB hard covering that forms over a wound when it is healing

SLIME slippery substance released by some animals

WART small and hard lump on the skin

DISCUSS

1. Sanna makes gross food for Birdy and Cassie in her cauldron. What's the grossest food you've eaten?

2. Cassie helps Birdy survive Sanna's evil plans. Do you think Birdy would have been able to win without her?

3. Ranger Dan doesn't find out about Sanna's plot until the end of the story. Do you think he would have helped if Birdy and Cassie told him what was happening?

WRITE

1. Cassie overhears Sanna talking to her assistants about using Birdy for her spell. Write about what would have happened if Cassie hadn't heard her. Do you think Birdy still would have found a way to escape?

2. Birdy has to use magic to hide from Sanna and fight her. Write a scene where Birdy and Cassie have to hide in a mountain range near some campsites to escape Sanna. What could Birdy turn them into to blend in?

3. Sanna gets lost in the woods at the end of the story. Write about what would happen if Sanna came back for revenge. How would Birdy and Cassie get away from her this time?

AUTHOR

BENJAMIN HARPER has worked as an editor at Lucasfilm Ltd and DC Comics. He has written many books, including the Bug Girl series, *Obsessed with Star Wars* and *Rolling with BB-8*. He lives in California, USA, where he gardens, keeps butterflies and collects giant robots.

ILLUSTRATOR

TIMOTHY BANKS is an award-winning artist and illustrator from South Carolina, USA. He's created character designs for Nike, Nickelodeon and Cartoon Network, quirky covers for *Paste* magazine and lots of children's books with titles such as *There's a Norseman in My Classroom* and *The Frankenstein Journals*.

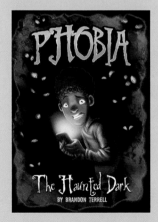

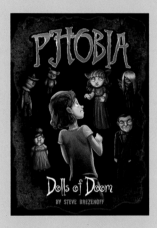

raintree

a Capstone company — publishers for children